Short stories

Voyage

1

Edited by
Chris Buckton and Pie Corbett

OXFORD
UNIVERSITY PRESS

OXFORD
UNIVERSITY PRESS

Great Clarendon Street, Oxford OX2 6DP

Oxford University Press is a department
of the University of Oxford.
It furthers the University's objective of excellence in
research, scholarship,and education by publishing
worldwide in

Oxford New York

Auckland   Cape Town   Dar es Salaam
Hong Kong   Karachi   Kuala Lumpur   Madrid
Melbourne   Mexico City   Nairobi   New Delhi
Shanghai   Taipei   Toronto

With offices in

Argentina   Austria   Brazil   Chile   Czech Republic
France   Greece   Guatemala   Hungary   Italy   Japan
Poland   Portugal   Singapore   South Korea   Switzerland
Thailand   Turkey   Ukraine   Vietnam

Oxford is a registered trade mark of Oxford University
Press in the UK and in certain other countries

This selection © Oxford University Press 2005

Database right Oxford University Press (maker)

First published 2005

British Library Cataloguing in Publication Data

Data available

ISBN 0 19 834966 1

ISBN 978 019 834966 2

10 9 8 7 6 5 4 3 2 1

Printed in Hong Kong

Acknowledgements

Cover illustration by Andy Parker

Illustrations by: David Semple pp 4–7; Bee Willey c/o
Illustration Ltd pp9–12; Pesky Kids c/o Apple Agency
pp14–17; Jess Mikhail pp19–22; Greg Becker c/o Illustration
Ltd pp23–25; Sholto Walker c/o Illustration Ltd pp27, 28,
59, 60, 62, 63; Linda Bronson c/o Illustration Ltd pp30–33;
Martin Chatterton pp34–37; Mike Spoor pp39, 41–44, 46,
47, 49–51; Pesky Kids c/o Apple Agency pp53, 55–58.

We are grateful to those who have kindly given permission
for use of the following copyright material.

Susan Price: 'The Princess and the Pea' from *The Kingfisher
Treasury of Nursery Stories* selected and retold by Susan Price
(Kingfisher, 1990), text © Susan Price 1990, reprinted by
permission of A M Heath & Co Ltd.

Philippa Werry: 'The Day Michael Made the News', ©
Philippa Werry 1993, first published by Learning Media Ltd
in *School Journal 1:3*, 1993 on behalf of the Ministry of
Education, reprinted by permission of the author and
Learning Media Ltd, New Zealand.

Ursula Wölfel: 'The Night Bird' translated by Gordon
Fielden from *The Light and the Dark: Stories to Think About* (The
Lutterworth Press, 1972), reprinted by permission of the
publishers.

Other stories in this collection are published here for the
first time by permission of their authors.

Rachel Anderson: 'Caleb's Clobber', © Rachel Anderson
2005.

Elaine Canham: 'Mr Wolf', © Elaine Canham 2005.

Pie Corbett, 'The Boy Who Cried Wolf', 'The Wolf in
Sheep's Clothing', © Pie Corbett 2005.

Alan Gibbons: 'A Light in the Darkness', 'Old Nick's
Knife', © Alan Gibbons 2005.

Helena Pielichaty: 'Do-It-Yourself Story', © Helena
Pielichaty 2005.

Steve Barlow and Steve Skidmore: 'Moving Pictures', 'A
Light in the Darkness' © Steve Barlow and Steve Skidmore
2005.

Contents

THE DAY MICHAEL MADE THE NEWS

Once there was a boy called Michael, whose family only liked watching TV. They watched TV at breakfast, and after school, and during dinner, and before bed.

Michael liked going to the park to play football or cricket, but his dad only liked sport on TV.

Michael liked going to the zoo to look at the animals, but his mum only liked nature programmes on TV.

Michael liked playing games and making models, but his brother and sister only liked game shows on TV.

One day, Michael was walking home after playing football when he heard a lot of shouting coming from the post office.

There was a bang, and another bang, and a scream, and a crash.

A man with a mask over his face, and a bag in his hand, rushed out of the post office and jumped into a car. The car sped off, nearly knocking over two old men and a boy on a bike.

Michael's eyes were nearly popping out of his head, but he wrote down the car's number plate on the back of his hand.

Lots of people came out of the other shops, and next minute the police arrived, and the TV crews.

When the police asked if anyone had noticed the number on the number plate, everyone shook their heads. Then Michael stepped forward shyly, and told them that he had written it down.

The police were very pleased. "Well done!" they said, and they took him for a ride in the police car to the police station, and then they took him home.

Michael hoped his family would see him drive up in a real police car, but everyone was inside watching TV.

"Mum! Dad! Everyone!" he shouted as he came in the front door. "Guess what happened! Guess where I've been!"

"Hush! Shush!" they all said. "We're watching the news!"

"*I've* got some news," said Michael. "I was just walking home, and –"

"Look at that!" exclaimed his dad, still watching the TV screen. "Someone tried to rob the post office down the road!"

"That's what I'm telling you," Michael said. "I was walking past, and –"

"They fired two shots!" his mum called out. "Just fancy that!"

"I *heard* them," Michael said. "Then the man came running out –"

"The robber ran out and got into a waiting car," said his sister. "Quiet, Michael, I want to hear what happened next."

7

"I'll tell you," said Michael. "The car drove off, and –"

"Someone wrote down the car's number," said Michael's brother. "That was quick thinking."

"It was *me*," Michael shouted. "*I* wrote it down. Look, there I am on TV!"

Sure enough, there was his face filling up the whole screen, and his voice telling the TV reporter what had happened.

"That boy looks just like Michael!" cried his mother, and his father, and his sister, and his brother.

They all turned round to look at him.

"Where have you been, Michael?" asked his mother. "You're very late home."

"I'll tell you," said Michael. "If you'll only *listen*."

And, for once, they did.

Philippa Werry

The Night Bird

There was once a boy who was always very frightened whenever he had to stay in the flat alone at night. His parents often went out in the evening, and then the boy was so frightened that he couldn't get to sleep.

He could hear something rustling: it was as if there was someone in the room, breathing.

He heard a creak and a groan: it sounded as if there was something moving about under his bed.

But the worst thing of all was the Night Bird.

The boy could always see it sitting out there on the window-sill. It never moved except when a car went past down below, and then it would flap its wings and the boy could see the huge shadow they made on the ceiling of his room.

The boy told his parents about being afraid. But all they said was: "Don't be a baby! You're just imagining it all." And they still went on going out in the evening. They couldn't see the bird and they didn't take the story seriously.

Then once when the boy was alone again the doorbell rang.

The boy went rigid with fear.

It rang again.

It rang and rang.

And then it stopped and for a long time everything was quiet.

Then something began to scratch at the wall of the house. The Night Bird! Now it was climbing up the wall with its long claws. Now it had reached the window-sill. And now it was banging on the window with its beak! Once, twice, over and over again, louder and louder – and soon the glass would break and the Bird would come leaping into the room!

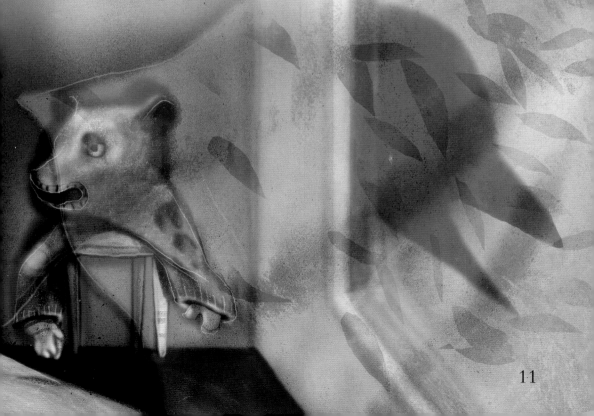

The boy grabbed the flower vase from the table near his bed and hurled it at the window.

The glass shattered. There was a rush of wind into the room so that the curtain blew high up against the wall. And the Bird was gone.

In the street below the boy heard his mother and father calling.

He raced into the hall and in the dark found the light switch straight away, and the button that opened the downstairs door. Then he tore open the door of the flat and ran to meet his parents.

He laughed out loud, he was so glad that they were there. But they began to scold him. Their smart evening clothes were soaked with water from the flower vase.

"What on earth is going on?" demanded his father. "Now the window's broken!"

"And just look at my coat!" cried his mother.

"The Night Bird was at the window," said the boy. "The Night Bird was pecking at the window with his beak."

"Rubbish!" said his father. "We'd forgotten our key and you didn't hear the bell. That's why we banged on your window with a pole from the building site."

"But it was the Night Bird, really!" said the boy. "It was the Night Bird!"

But his parents didn't understand. They still went on going out in the evening, leaving the boy alone.

He was still afraid and he still heard the rustling and the creaking and the groaning. But that was not so bad.

Because the Night Bird never came back. He had driven it away. He had driven it away all by himself.

Ursula Wölfel

Caleb's Clobber

Caleb had loads of clothes. He kept them in a box under the bunk-bed. They were not new. All Caleb's clobber was passed down from his big brothers and sisters.

Caleb liked wearing their friendly old rugby shirts, outgrown sweaters, faded socks. He even quite liked his sisters' hand-me-down pyjamas with the rabbit pattern. But he did sometimes wonder what it felt like to wear something quite new, which you'd never seen before on somebody else.

When Caleb's eldest brother, Craig, was picked for the Under 13's he got new football boots. Caleb asked him what they felt like. Craig just shrugged. "Nothing special. Things never stay new for long."

One day, Caleb was invited to his mate Mike's birthday party. On the card it said:

Caleb thought about this. What should he wear? An old rugby shirt was casual but not sharp. Rabbit pyjamas were wacky but definitely not cool.

For the first time ever, Caleb wished he had something new to wear.

Soon, all the brothers and sisters knew about his wishing. Craig said to Cally who said it to Clive who said it to Celia, "Caleb never gets new clothes."

So, on pocket-money day there was a lot of whispering and clinking of coins.

Caleb said, "What's up?"

"Shopping trip."

"Can I come?"

"No," said Celia.

"Sorry," said Clive.

"It's private," said Cally.

"You'll see soon enough," said Craig.

And in a while, Caleb did. Craig handed him a parcel. Inside was a brand-new Hawaiian shirt, patterned with purple palm trees.

"Cool!" said Caleb. "Wacky or what!"

Then Cally gave him a gift-wrapped packet. Inside was a rainbow-striped baseball cap.

"Wow!" said Caleb. "Sharp."

Then Clive gave him a bag. Inside was a spotted sock. Mint fresh. "For your right foot," said Clive.

Celia handed Caleb the other spotted sock, but not in a bag. "For your left foot."

"Cool!" said Caleb. "Spotty socks."

Caleb went off to Mike's party looking the coolest dude in town. He had a great time.

But when he came home, he raced straight upstairs and took off the cap, the shirt, the left sock and the right. He put on the faded rugby shirt, the worn sweater, the friendly old socks.

"Hm, that's better," he thought. "Now I feel more like me."

"Hey Caleb!" called Craig and Cally, Clive and Celia. "What's happened to your new stuff?"

"It's in my box under the bed. I'm keeping it so it stays new forever."

Rachel Anderson

Do-It-Yourself Story

Dear Reader,

Thank you so much for reading my story. I'm sure you'll like it. It's very good. There is just one teeny, tiny problem. It isn't quite ready yet.

I have done all the main bits, but I just don't have time to finish it. You see, I am in the middle of making a Tuna Pasta Bake for dinner, and if I stop to finish the story the cheese sauce will go lumpy – yuck! So would you mind adding a few bits to the story yourself?

Here's what I have got so far. There's a girl in it called Raven. She looks a bit like that girl you know in Year Five who plays the recorder. There's a boy in it called Bill who always forgets his swimming stuff and eats with his mouth open. They are the two main characters. You can choose how old they are

me

HOME
sweet
HOME

lumpy
cheese
sauce

but they mustn't be older than eleven or younger than six, OK?

There is also a dog in the story, but there is no cat. I don't really like cats, to be honest. I did like the one who played Puss in Boots in *Shrek 2*, though. Now he was funny. If all cats were *that* funny, I might use them in my stories more.

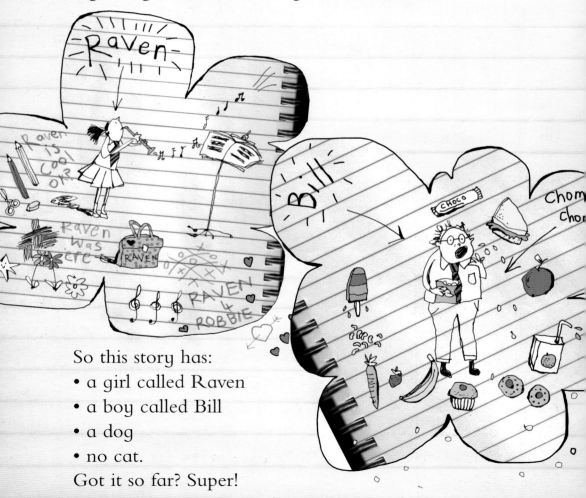

So this story has:
• a girl called Raven
• a boy called Bill
• a dog
• no cat.
Got it so far? Super!

In the story, Raven and Bill have a fight one lunchtime. The fight gets so bad that one of the dinner ladies has to come and sort them out. Here is a little bit of conversation from that part of the story. Do feel free to add more.

"Stop it at once or you'll be sent to Mr Green," the *dinner lady bellowed.*

The dinner lady is called Mrs Cook which is funny when you think about it (but not as funny as that cat in *Shrek 2*). Mrs Cook is as tall and thin as a bull-rush. Her hair is cropped short and dyed purple and she wears spotty socks. (I thought I'd tell you that so you can draw a splendid picture of her for me. I haven't found a proper illustrator for my story yet, so if you want the job, it's yours). Oh, and give her some rosy cheeks when you draw her. I do like a dinner lady with rosy cheeks.

Dinner lady

"Stop it at once or you'll be sent to Mr Green."

TOMATO SAUCE

Spotty Socks

Anyway, Raven and Bill don't listen to Mrs Cook. They are too busy pushing and shoving each other and shouting things like, "I never touched your stupid lunch box, you big fibber." So Mrs Cook calls for Mr Green, the headmaster.

Now, Mr Green is one very scary guy. Even the hair growing from his nose carries a white flag that says: "Help, get me out of here!"

When Mrs Cook tells Mr Green about the fight, Mr Green is furious. And I mean furious. Big Time. "Send them to me at once," he says in a deep, gruff voice.

Anyway, that's as far as I've got, so if you could finish the story off for me, I'd be so grateful. I really must get back to my Tuna Pasta Bake before those lumps appear. Oh, and don't forget to bring the dog into the story, will you? It'll be barking mad otherwise. Thanks ever so much.

With very best wishes,

Helena

Helena Pielichaty

The Boy Who Cried "Wolf!"

Everyone knows that wolves are dangerous. They hunt in packs and it is not only lambs that they kill. Everyone knows about the wolf that chased Little Red Riding Hood and tried to eat the three pigs. Everyone knows that wolves are not cuddly toys for playtime…

Once upon a time there was a young shepherd boy whose job it was to look after the villagers' flock of sheep. Every morning, he took the flock onto the mountainside. Every evening, he brought them home again. But during the day there was not much to do – the sheep chewed the grass, the lambs bleated at each other and the ram slept. The boy grew bored.

Now they do say that the devil makes mischief for idle hands, and this time he certainly stirred up a cauldron of trouble. For the boy decided to play a trick. He dashed down the hillside, shouting, "Wolf! Wolf!" At once, all the villagers rushed out to protect their flock.

The boy hid behind a rock and laughed at the burly baker, the blacksmith, the red-faced butcher and the women as they all ran up the hill shouting and waving their arms to chase off a wolf that did not exist. In fact, he thought it was so amusing that he did it several times. Each time he pretended that the wolf had run away. It wasn't long before the villagers decided that he was tricking them.

Now tricks turn to trouble, as sure as snow melts in the sun, for one day a pack of wolves *did* come stalking out of the forest. They had eyes of fire and were so thin that their ribs showed through their fur. The boy ducked down behind a rock. He screamed and he screamed, "Wolf! Wolf!" But no one came.

The blacksmith paused with his hammer raised high. He listened to the boy's distant screams, and just shook his head. Then he struck another blow on the anvil, sending sparks flying. The women in the fields tut-tutted and carried on with their work. And the baker muttered, "That's the shepherd boy, up to his tricks!" So they all ignored the boy's screams.

Later that day, the shepherd boy returned to the village on his own. There were no sheep following, no lambs bleating for their mothers. Just silence, for the wolves had taken all the sheep – and left the shepherd boy feeling sheepish. He had played the fool once too often and now he had made a fool of himself.

Moral of the tale: If you keep on lying then in the end no one will believe you – even if you are telling the truth.

Pie Corbett

The Wolf In Sheep's Clothing

Once upon a time there was a sly wolf. He was skinny as a snake and hungry for meat.

One day the wolf saw a flock of sheep on the hillside. There was snow on the ground and it was very cold. A shepherd was busy, feeding the sheep. He called them by their names and even patted their backs. The shepherd cared for his flock — but to the wolf they were nothing more than lamb chops.

Later that day, the wolf was out hunting on the snowy mountainside when he found a sheepskin. The wolf felt his belly rumble.

At that moment he had an idea. Perhaps he could dress up as a sheep and join the flock! The shepherd would never see through such a disguise and the wolf could eat the sheep one by one without anyone knowing.

In the evening, when the sun was setting and the shadows grew tall, the wolf slipped out of the forest. He was dressed in the sheepskin. A few of the sheep bleated when they saw him. But they were tired and cold. All they wanted was the warmth of their pen.

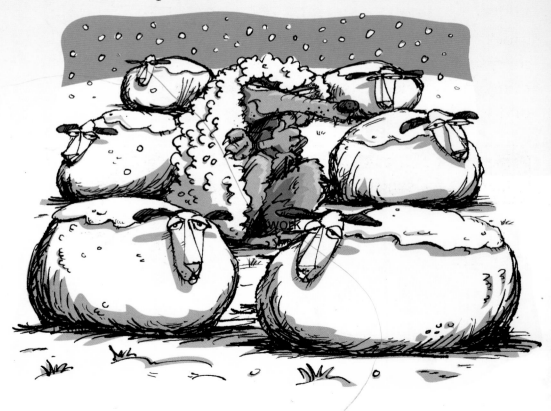

That night the wolf snuggled down with the sheep. He was surrounded by more Sunday dinners than he could imagine!

But the wolf's plan was not as clever as he had hoped.

The shepherd and his wife wanted some meat for their dinner. So the shepherd went down to the pen and selected the thinnest looking sheep. Then he killed it for his wife to roast on the fire. But it was not a sheep that he had killed. It was the wolf!

The good shepherd and his wife had quite a shock when they saw the dead wolf with the sheepskin pulled over its body. The shepherd thanked his lucky stars that he had killed the wolf and saved the rest of the flock.

Moral of the tale: it is not a good idea to pretend that you are something that you are not.

Pie Corbett

The Princess and The Pea

Once upon a time there was a Prince, and he wanted to marry a Princess; but she had to be a *real* Princess. He travelled all over the world in his search for a Princess, and Princesses he found in plenty; but whether they were *real* Princesses he couldn't decide, for now one thing, now another, seemed not quite right. At last he returned home to his palace and was very sad, because he wished so much to have a real Princess for his wife.

One evening there was a fearful storm; thunder crashed, lightning flashed, rain poured down from the sky in torrents – and it was dark as dark can be. All at once there was heard a knocking at the door. The Prince's father, the old King himself, went out to open it.

A Princess stood outside; but gracious! What a sight she was, out there in the rain. Water trickled down from her hair; water dripped from her clothes; water ran in at the toes of her shoes and out at the heels. And yet she said she was a real Princess.

"We shall soon see about that!" thought the old Queen, but she didn't say anything.

She went into the bedroom, took all the clothes off the bed and laid one dried pea on the mattress. Then she piled twenty more mattresses on top of it, and twenty eiderdowns over that. On this the girl who said she was a real Princess was to lie all night.

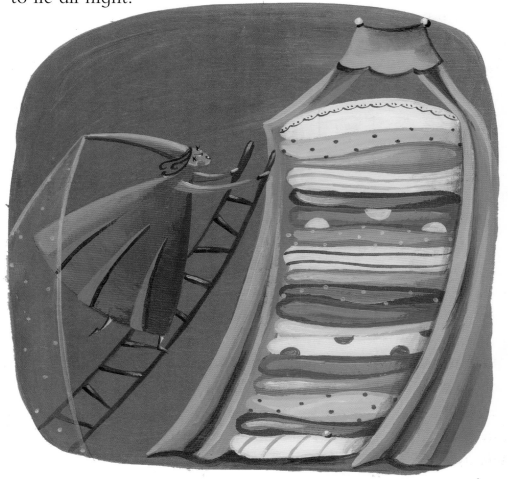

The next morning she was asked how she had slept.

"Oh, shockingly!" she replied. "I haven't even closed my eyes. I don't know what was in my bed, but there was something hard that has bruised me all over."

They saw at once that she must be a *real* Princess, for she had felt the little dried pea through twenty eiderdowns and twenty mattresses. Only a *real* Princess could have such delicate skin.

So the Prince asked the Princess to marry him, and the pea was put in a museum, as a curiosity. You may go yourself and see it.

Now, wasn't that a *real* story?

Hans Christian Andersen,
retold by **Susan Price**

Mr Wolf

Once upon a time there was a little girl who was very kind but not very bright. She liked to go to her granny's house every week with a basket full of cakes she baked herself. Mostly she went by bus, but one day she decided to bike through the dark, dark woods on the council's new cycle path, so that she could spend her bus fare on an extra treat for her granny. As she whizzed along, a wolf, who was big, bad, and very hungry, looked at her and licked his chops.

"Mmmm," he thought. "Meals on Wheels."

But while he was thinking, the little girl had already passed him, and he had to run to catch her up.

Soon he was loping beside her shiny new bicycle.

"Hello, Mr Wolf," she said brightly, still pedalling quite fast.

Mr Wolf didn't say anything. He hadn't had any exercise for a long time and all this running was making him breathless.

Finally she came to a stop outside her granny's house. As she dropped her bike on the path, Mr Wolf slunk round the back of the house and climbed in through a window. He was very tired.

"Hello, Mr Wolf," said the little girl's granny. "What can I do for you?"

Mr Wolf was so tired he could hardly speak. "I've come to eat you, Gran," he wheezed.

"Come to meet me?" said the granny. "That's nice." And she shook his paw so hard he yelped.

"Granny!" called the little girl, coming into the house. Mr Wolf hid behind the door, but the little girl opened it so hard, it banged his nose.

And as she ran towards her grandmother she stepped on his tail.

"Aaaaahhooooeeeeeee!!!!!" yelled the wolf. "My tail!"

"Ah," said Granny. "We'll put a packet of frozen peas on it. That'll make it better." She tugged at the door of the freezer but it wouldn't open. The little girl tugged at it too, but it still wouldn't open.

"Here," snarled Mr Wolf, hopping from one paw to another and holding his nose at the same time. "You stupid old woman. Let me." But he tugged the door of the freezer so hard the whole thing fell on him and squashed him flat.

Granny looked at the little girl. "Oh dear," she said. "I must ask Mr Huntsman – you know, that man who has the big axe – to come and lift up my freezer. He'll get Mr Wolf out."

But before she could even pull her mobile phone out of her apron pocket Mr Wolf had pushed the freezer away and was running out of the front door.

"Well I never," exclaimed the granny.

"Ooh, watch out!" shouted the little girl as Mr Wolf tripped over her bike and scraped his legs.

"Come back soon!" called the granny. "We'd love to have you for tea sometime!"

Elaine Canham

A Light In The Darkness

Cass first saw the light just before bedtime on Tuesday night, about nine o'clock. It didn't shine for long, just a moment, like a silver disc. Then it was gone.

"Did you see that?" she asked her twin sister Kate.

All Kate did was grunt from the other side of the room. She was tired after a hard day hogging the computer.

"I saw a light," Cass said. "It was out there, just beyond the back fence."

Kate said she was seeing things, and that was that. At least it was until the light flashed again and a shadow crossed it.

"You must have seen that!" Cass said.

But Kate hadn't. By Wednesday night, Cass was desperate to prove she really had seen something. She just wouldn't let Kate go to sleep.

"Why don't we keep watch?" Cass said. "Just for an hour."

"I'm not sitting at the window for an hour," Kate said. "People will think we're weird."

"Who's going to see us?" Cass asked. "There's nothing at the back, just fields."

Kate had no answer to that, so they watched.

"See," Kate said after half an hour. "Nothing. You're seeing things."

"It's only just nine," said Cass.

"So? Kate said. "Nothing's going to happen."

But, just as she was about to turn away from the window, the light flashed, just once, like an eye winking.

"There!" said Cass. "You saw that, didn't you?"

"It's somebody with a torch," said Kate.

"Nonsense, that light is far too big to be a torch."

And it was. At this distance it had to be as big as a football, maybe bigger.

The twins told their parents what they'd seen. Dad had an explanation.

"There was a factory there once," he said. "Or

a warehouse or something. It'll be an old piece of metal flashing in the street lights."

That didn't convince the twins. The light was a perfect circle.

"It could be a ghost, or maybe even light from a spaceship," said Cass.

"Don't be stupid," said Kate.

"What then?"

"I don't know, but there's got to be a better explanation than that."

The next morning they went to see.

"There's nothing here," said Cass, disappointed.

But Kate thought they were looking in the wrong place. They stood in line with their bedroom window and looked around.

"It's got to be further back," said Kate.

That's when they saw it, a round metal cover half hidden by the grass.

"It can't be that," Cass said. "It's all rusty. It wouldn't flash."

"No," said Kate. "But if the light came from down there..."

Cass caught on.

"You'd see it when somebody lifted the cover."

The twins tried to lift the cover but it was too heavy. It didn't matter. Cass had an idea. Just under their window was the garden security light. If they hung something out of the window in front of the light, they would set it off. With the light on, they would be able to see who was lifting the cover.

So that's what they did. Just after nine that night the light flashed. Immediately they swung a pillow case in front of the security light.

"Down!" Cass gasped.

Illuminated by the security light was a man about to climb into whatever lay below the metal cover.

"Why's somebody going down there?" Kate whispered as she dropped to the floor.

Cass shrugged and stole a look outside. The man hesitated, then must have decided the light was nothing to worry about. He disappeared underground.

"I don't know," Cass said. "But I think we should tell."

Tell they did. Within an hour everything had gone mad.

"Hang on," said Mum. "There was something in today's paper." She waved it in front of Dad. The headline read: "Don't approach this man." Without a word of explanation the twins were packed off to bed. Soon sirens were screeching. Men's voices came from downstairs. The twins stared at each other. What was going on? Then, through the window they saw lights stabbing through the darkness. There were police cars parked outside and shadowy figures were moving, training flashlights on the ground.

The twins got to find out the truth half an hour later. Unable to stand it any longer they crept downstairs.

"You can come in," Dad said with a smile. "The excitement's all over."

He explained that an escaped prisoner had been hiding out in the basement of the old, demolished factory. He'd been stupid enough to leave a light on in the basement when he went out at night. The police had taken him away in handcuffs. Mum said he would be locked away for years.

In stories, the kids who catch the bad guy get a reward. It didn't happen in real life. All that Mum said was, "That could have been really dangerous, girls! Promise me you'll never go off investigating things again. And stay away from strangers!" She gave the twins an enormous hug.

"Now bed! Time to get some sleep."

As if it were that easy!

Alan Gibbons

Old Nick's Knife

Suddenly this doesn't seem such a good idea.

"Are you sure we shouldn't go back?" I ask Lee.

He does his dumb chicken impression. It means I'm a coward.

"Look," I say, "I'm not scared. I just think we should leave it until a better day."

I'm squinting against the whipping snowflakes. The air is icy. It bites into you like teeth of steel. All I've got on is my hoodie and I'm freezing.

"What's up?" Lee says. "Are you backing out?"

I don't answer. He's a good mate but I can't stand the way he winds me up all the time.

"You said you'd climb Old Nick's Knife in the dark," he teases.

"Yes," I say. "But that was before the snow came down."

Already the path is covered in snow. Old Nick's Knife is the ridge a few hundred yards from our estate. Dad says it used to be a slag heap from when they had coal mines round here. It towers above the houses like some dark monster. And the drop, it's like a cliff face. The path has to wind round and round to reach the top. Right now the wind is roaring in our faces and I want to go home.

"Lee," I say. "This is stupid."

"Not as stupid as you if you give up." He does the chicken noise again. "Besides, we're halfway already."

It's going dark. I'm starting to think it might be better to get to the top and come home the long way.

"OK," I say. "We carry on. But we go home down Hill Road."

He shrugs and we climb on. It's getting harder. The snowflakes are getting bigger and they're swirling round us like a shoal of white fish. If Mum and Dad knew where I was, they'd kill me. Old Nick's Knife is out of bounds but there are loads of places where you can get through the fence. I'm still picturing myself crawling through the safety fence when I slip. Bam! Smack on my face like a baby seal. Lee shrieks with laughter but the wind shrieks louder. I just see his mouth wide open.

"Let's get to the top," I grumble. "Then we can go home."

The last few steps are hard. I feel a wrenching yank on my sleeve. It's Lee slithering backwards. In spite of the cold I see beads of sweat on his forehead. The path is narrower here. I pull him towards me and yell against the wind.

"See, I told you this was stupid."

Lee doesn't say anything for a few moments. He's just understood how dangerous the climb is.

"OK," he says, staring into the howling blackness below us. "We plant the banner and we take the long way home."

This is his big idea. We made our banner. It's just an old sheet painted with our names and fastened to two poles. Lee's been clinging to it all the way up. Next to our names it says: "We climbed Old Nick's Knife."

I've told Lee nobody will be able to see it but he doesn't care.

"The point is," he keeps telling me, "*we'll* know what it says."

We finally scramble to the top. It's hard to keep our footing.

"Get away from the edge," I pant.

Lee just laughs and makes his chicken noise, but he comes anyway.

"Hammer," he says.

I pull out the hammer I took from the shed. Lee plants the poles in the snow and I start pounding them in.

"It's hard," I tell him. "The ground's frozen."

Lee's about to say something when it happens. The wind booms across the snow and the banner fills like a parachute. Lee screams as it whips him off his feet. It fills, billowing out with a loud snap. Worse still it spins Lee round and starts to drag him towards the edge.

"No!"

I make a grab for him and wrap my fingers round his wrist. Now I'm being dragged too. I scramble to get a grip on the snow.

"The banner," I yell. "Let it go."

Lee does as he's told. It whips into the dark, a spinning white bird swooping up then out into the blackness. It doesn't stop him slithering over the edge. I tug hard but I'm still sliding after him.

"Do something!" he screams.

His legs are kicking over emptiness. Still I'm skidding over the snow. That's when I feel the hammer in my other hand. I punch the claw end into the ground. Still I'm slipping.

"Please!"

Raising my arm I beat down again with the hammer. This time it bites.

How long we lie there I don't know, but in the end we manage to squirm and wriggle our way to safety. With arms and legs like jelly we struggle to firmer ground. We're halfway down Hill Road when Lee stops me. I can see the lights of home winking up ahead.

"Thanks," he says. "You were right. That was stupid." He gives a nervous half-smile. "Sorry."

I smile. It will be a while before he calls me chicken again.

Alan Gibbons

MOVING PICTURES

Monica ran her fingers along the shelves. "Plastic spiders, itching powder, fake blood … *fantastic!*"

She grinned. This shop had the lot. Stink bombs, foaming sugar, whoopee cushions. Everything you'd ever need for playing the most brilliant jokes.

An old, grey haired man appeared. His round face broke into a smile. "Hello," he said. "Do you like practical jokes?"

"Oh yes!" said Monica. "I'm the biggest joker in our class. I saw your sign on the way to school – *Old Nick's Joke Shop* – and I just had to come in! Are you Old Nick?"

The old man laughed. "Indeed I am. And just for you, I've got the best joke in the world. You'll have fun with this."

Monica whooped. "Wicked!"

"That's exactly right." Old Nick reached into a drawer and brought out a pencil. "It's yours for fifty pence."

"It doesn't look very funny," said Monica. "What does it do?"

"Aha!" said Old Nick mysteriously. "Try it and find out."

Later that morning it was art class. Monica's teacher had put an apple on the table, and everyone was getting ready to draw it.

Monica got out her new pencil and opened her sketchpad. As she picked up the pencil, it seemed to tug at her hand. Before she knew it, the pencil started drawing the apple! Colours began to flow - red, then green, then brown. Seconds later there was the most amazingly lifelike picture of an apple.

As Monica stared in disbelief, the apple fell out of the picture and into her lap! Only the outline of the fruit remained on the page.

Monica picked up the apple and grinned. Old Nick was right – she'd have some wicked fun with this pencil!

She wondered what joke she could play. She noticed Andy sitting in front of her. Smiling, Monica began to draw.

Once again the pencil took over. Within seconds, a big fat green wriggly frog hopped off the page. Monica carefully picked it up, leaned forward and dropped it down the back of Andy's neck. Andy's eyes bulged. Then he started screaming and leaping about the classroom.

Eventually the frog dropped out of Andy's trouser leg and was captured. The teacher eyed Monica. "Where did that come from?" she asked.

"I didn't bring it in," replied Monica. Which was true, but not totally honest.

That day was the best day Monica had ever spent at school. By the time the final bell rang, there'd been a flock of sheep in the staff room, giant spiders in the boys' toilets and a chimpanzee in the playground.

But as Monica headed home, she met Andy and his big sister at the school gate.

"You played a nasty joke on my brother," said Andy's sister. "Your joking days are over."

Monica whipped out her sketchpad and the pencil. "Be careful. I'm armed!"

"With a pencil?" scoffed Andy's sister.

"Yes, I'm quick on the draw!"

Monica scribbled furiously. In seconds, an enormous Tyrannosaurus Rex stepped out of the page. Its huge feet thudded onto the pavement. It fixed Andy and his sister with a beady eye, and roared.

Andy and his sister ran off screaming. Monica laughed like anything. But then the Tyrannosaurus turned towards her.

Monica stopped laughing and ran for her life.

She raced through the town, with the beast close behind her. Cars swerved and people looked on in terror. An idea popped into her head – the joke shop! Maybe Old Nick could help.

Putting on a final spurt, Monica skidded round a corner and into the shop. Old Nick looked up.

"Help me!" cried Monica. "There's a Tyrannosaurus Rex outside! How can I stop it?"

"Ah," said Old Nick wisely. "It's easier to start things than to stop them."

Then Monica had a brilliant idea.

"A magic pencil got me into this mess," she said. "Maybe a magic eraser could get me out of it. Do you have one?"

Old Nick's eyes narrowed. "Yes, I have one of those."

Monica sighed with relief. She pulled out a fifty pence piece from her pocket.

Old Nick shook his head. Suddenly, he didn't seem so friendly. There was a red glow in his eyes.

"Magic *pencils* are fifty pence," he said. He gave a horrible laugh. "Magic *erasers* are a *lot* more expensive...."

Steve Barlow and *Steve Skidmore*

Knight Time

"Mum," said Josh, "Who was the wizard who helped King Arthur?"

Mum's brush slipped and a big dollop of paint fell to the floor.

"Oh, Josh! You're always asking questions." Mum rubbed at the paint with a cloth, making a smear. "Go away and stop bothering me!"

Josh went outside. His dad was fixing the car.

"Dad," said Josh, "Who was the wizard who helped King Arthur?"

His dad dropped a spanner on his toe. "Questions, questions, questions!" he groaned. "Go away, Josh. I'm busy."

Josh went through the garden and out of the gate. He wandered up the path, into the woods. The wizard's name was on the tip of his tongue; he just couldn't quite remember it. Josh sighed. He was always getting in trouble for asking questions. Maybe he should stop…

"Halt!" Josh looked up. Standing in the middle of the path, right in front of him, was a knight. He was dressed in shining armour and riding a great war-horse.

"Er, hello?" said Josh.

"Kneel!" cried the knight.

Josh shook his head. "My name isn't Neil, it's Josh."

The knight ignored this. "I have lost my way in this enchanted forest." He stared through a gap in the trees. "I see smoke from a town. It must be Camelot."

"No," said Josh, "it's Crawley."

The knight looked up, startled, as a jet airliner roared overhead. "A fire breathing dragon," he roared, "from the Mountains of Doom!"

"It's a jumbo jet," said Josh, "from Gatwick airport." But he was talking to himself. The knight was galloping down the path, waving his lance and shouting battle cries.

The aeroplane vanished in the distance and the knight came back. "See how the foul beast flies from me!" he cried.

"But it *wasn't* a dragon." Josh told him. "Why don't you *ask* if you don't know what it is…?"

Just then, Josh heard the rattling, rasping noise of a motorbike engine. He looked down the path. A motorcyclist was roaring towards him, on a trail bike. He was dressed in a crash helmet and black leathers. There was a girl sitting behind him.

"The Black Knight!" snapped a voice from behind Josh. "He is kidnapping yon fair damsel!" Josh jumped to one side as the knight spurred his horse past.

"No!" cried Josh. "It's Big Dave from the farm!
He's taking his girlfriend for a spin!" But the
knight rode on. Big Dave gawped at the maniac
galloping towards him. He gave a hoarse cry and
sped back the way he'd come.

Josh watched the knight canter back. What a
know-all! He never asked questions, he thought
he knew everything, and he was always wrong.

"Look," said Josh kindly, "I reckon you're stuck
in the wrong time. If you see something you don't
understand, just ask me, and…"

"I am a knight," said the knight proudly.
"Knights do not *ask*, they *know*!"

Just then, Josh's mobile phone rang. He took it out of his pocket.

"Aha!" cried the knight, "Thou art a wizard!"

"No!" Josh was getting fed up. "It's just a text – from my friend Mervyn…"

"Merlin?" howled the knight.

"Merlin! *That's* the name of King Arthur's wizard! I've remembered!" Josh was delighted.

"Merlin is my enemy!" The knight charged at Josh. "Have at thee, varlet!"

"Ooer!" Josh ran for dear life. He pelted down the path with the knight getting nearer and nearer…

But as they reached the end of the woods, a train shot along the railway line at the bottom of the hill. It disappeared into a tunnel.

"Another dragon!" cried the knight. "I must challenge it."

"It's not a dragon!" shouted Josh, "Why don't you listen? It's…" But the knight rode straight past. Josh threw his hands in the air and gave up.

The knight's horse had more sense than its master. It wouldn't go into the tunnel. The knight dismounted. As Josh watched, he drew his sword and marched into the tunnel mouth.

From inside the tunnel came the 'Mneeeee-Mnaaaaaa!' of a train hooter. Josh stared as the knight's shield came spinning out of the tunnel like a frisbee, followed by the 4.15 to Brighton. Josh blinked. The horse and the shield had vanished. He hoped the knight had also gone back to wherever he had come from.

As Josh walked home, shaking his head, he decided that pretending you knew everything was really stupid. There was nothing wrong with asking questions. He was going to go on asking as many as he possibly could.

And sometimes, he'd even listen to the answers.

Steve Barlow and *Steve Skidmore*